WHERE ARE THE BEARS?

WHERE ARE THE BEARS?

Kay Winters

illustrated by
Brian Lies

A Yearling First Choice Chapter Book

Dedicated to Arlene Robbins,   *To Madeline*   *—BL*
who always believed,
with special thanks to Susan Korman
and Michelle Poploff   *—KW*

Published by
Bantam Doubleday Dell Publishing Group, Inc.
1540 Broadway
New York, New York 10036
Text copyright © 1998 by Kay Winters
Illustrations copyright © 1998 by Brian Lies

Library of Congress Cataloging-in-Publication Data
Winters, Kay.
  Where are the bears? / Kay Winters ; illustrated by Brian Lies.
    p. cm.
  "A Yearling first choice chapter book."
  Summary: Two bear cubs spy on some campers and explore their tent
while they are away.
  ISBN 0-385-32291-7 (alk. paper). —ISBN 0-440-41308-7 (pbk. : alk.
paper).
  [1. Bears—Fiction. 2. Camping—Fiction.]   I. Lies, Brian, ill. II. Title.
PZ7.W7675Wh   1998
[E]—dc20   96-34388
                                      CIP
                                      AC

Hardcover: The trademark Delacorte Press® is registered in the
U.S. Patent and Trademark Office and in other countries.
Paperback: The trademark Yearling® is registered in the
U.S. Patent and Trademark Office and in other countries.
The text of this book is set in 17-point Baskerville.
Book design by Trish Parcell Watts
Manufactured in the United States of America
July 1998
10 9 8 7 6 5 4 3

CONTENTS

1.
CAMPERS!

It was the first day of camping season.

Mother Bear spoke gruffly to her cubs.

"Campers are coming today."

"YES!" said Sassy.

"COOL!" said Lum.

"BEWARE!" said Mother Bear.

"You can never tell WHAT
campers will do."

The cubs ran to the lake to watch.
Soon cars stuffed with boxes,
bags, and campers
bumped slowly into the park.
One car had something big on top.
It pulled into a campsite.
The bear cubs waited.
"Here they are!" said Lum.

"At last!" said Sassy. "CAMPERS!"

"Don't let them see you," warned Lum.

"Remember what Mother said."

"POOH!" said Sassy.

"I'm not scared! I'm a BEAR!"

Three campers got out of the car.

"At last!" said the big camper.

"Cool!" said the small camper.

"I can't wait to see BEARS!"

The middle camper looked around.

"Hope not," she said. "Too scary!

You can never tell WHAT bears will do."

The big camper clapped his hands.

"Time to set up the tent," he said.

The middle one pulled something

out of the car.

"Let's put the tent here," she said.

"So that's a tent," whispered Sassy.

The cubs had heard about tents
from their mother.

"It's flat!" said Lum. "How funny!"

"Campers must crawl in," said Sassy.

"Hold the pole," said the big camper.

"Okay . . . LIFT!"

The tent went S L O W L Y up.

Bang! Clang! went the hammer.

The tent stood tall.

The campers cheered.

The bears stared.

"I have the sleeping bags,"
said the middle camper.

"Bring the pillows," she added.

The small camper took

three white lumps out of the car.

He threw one at the big camper.

The big camper threw it back.

Flip! Flop! Plop!

"Fun!" whispered Sassy to Lum.

"Let's put on our boots and go

for a hike," said the big camper.

"I'll take my camera,"
said the small one.
He pulled out a black box.
"I bet we'll see BEARS!"
"Better not!" said the middle one.
"I don't care for BEARS!"
The three campers hiked
down the trail.

2.
INTO THE TENT

"NOW!" said Sassy.

"What if they come back?" said Lum.

"Pooh!" said Sassy. "Come on!"

The bear cubs crept into the tent.

Lum lay down on a sleeping bag.

"MMMMM . . . soft!" he said.

He put his head on a white lump.

"What's this?" he asked.

"They called it a pillow," said Sassy.

She threw one at Lum.

He threw it back.

Flip! Flop! Plop!

Sassy threw again.

The pillow hit Lum on the nose.

He grabbed for it.

The claw in his paw ripped the pillow.

Feathers blew. Feathers flew.

"YIPES," he said.

"Now you did it," said Sassy.

Sassy tried to shut the tent flap.

She moved the silver thing up.

It was stuck.

"YIPES!" she said.

"Now YOU did it," said Lum.

Lum's head bumped the pole.

The tent leaned over and fell—

PLOP!—on top of them!

"OUCH!" he said.

"We're out of here!" said Sassy.

The bears crawled out of the tent.

They ran and hid in a tree.

"Hope Mother doesn't
find out," said Lum.
The campers came into sight.
"SOMEONE knocked over our tent!"
cried the small one.
"The wind?" said the big one.
"Look at these feathers!"
said the middle one.
The campers looked all around.
"I bet it was BEARS!"
the small one said.

3.
OUT ON THE LAKE

BANG! CLANG! Up went the tent again.
Just before sunset, the campers
slid something off the top of their car.
"We'll slide the boat down the bank,"
said the big one.

"Bring the oars," said the middle one.

The three campers climbed in.

They shoved off from the shore.

"So that's a boat!" said Lum.

"I want a ride," said Sassy.

"Not me!" said Lum.

"Too scary!"

The cubs saw the small camper
pull back and forth on the oars.

Soon the boat was far from shore.

"They're riding on water!" said Sassy.

"Too far out!" said Lum.

"POOH!" Sassy said. "Far out is fun!"

"Look at these funny things," said Lum.

Sassy picked up two hiking boots
set neatly together.

"Campers wear them on their paws,"
said Sassy. She tried on a pair.
Lum tasted his boot.
"Yuck!" he said, and threw it down.
The sun was setting.
The campers headed back to shore.
The small one tied the boat to a stump.
"Tie it tight," said the big camper.
"We don't want to lose the boat!"

"Look at our boots!"
said the middle camper.
"This is no time for tricks!"
said the big one.
"Don't look at me.
I didn't do it!" said the small one.

"SOMETHING has been here,"
he said. "And I know WHO!"
"You have bears on the brain,"
said the big one.
"Let's get the firewood."
The campers went into the woods.

4.
RIDING
ON WATER

"NOW!" said Sassy.

The two cubs slid down the bank.

Sassy got into the boat.

Lum just stood there.

"Come on!" said Sassy.

"Untie that rope and get in!"

Sassy pulled on the oars.

The boat shot ahead.

"Rowing is easy!" she said.

"Let me try," said Lum.

He stood up in the boat.

One oar slid into the lake.

"YIPES!" said Lum.

He reached for the oar.

SPLASH!

CRASH!

Both cubs fell into the lake.

The oars floated away.

The boat bobbed upside down.

"Now you did it!" said Sassy.

"Me? YOU!" said Lum.

Sassy splashed Lum.

Lum splashed back.

By now the sun had set.

Two soggy bear cubs made

their way to the shore.

The boat floated away.

The campers came back with firewood.

"What was all that splashing?"

said the middle one.

The small camper ran down the bank.

"SOMEONE took our boat!" he yelled.

"I told you to tie it tight!"
said the big one.
"But I did!" the small camper said.
"We'll look for it in the morning,"
said the middle camper.
"Those BEARS!" said the small one.

5.
THE CAMPFIRE

Later that night the bear cubs
saw the campers piling sticks in a heap.
"I'll light the fire," said the big camper.
"Marshmallows!" said the small one.
The campers put some white lumps
on sticks.
"Here come the raccoon twins,"
whispered Lum.

"They've heard about campers too."
The campers held sticks over the fire.
The marshmallows turned
black and gooey.
"Yum!" said the small one.
"Tell a spooky story," he begged.

The big one said,
"In a deep dark woods . . ."
The other two campers shivered.
When it was over, the middle one said,
"I'll get my guitar."
The campers howled together about
a bear who went over a mountain.

"Time for bed," said the big one.
"Bring your flashlights."
The campers brushed their teeth
at the pump.
Who who whooo, hooted the owl.
Sassy stepped on a tree branch.
Crackle! Snap!
"Shhh!" said Lum. "They'll hear us."

"POOH!" said Sassy. "Who cares?
I'm not scared of campers!"
"What's that?" said the middle camper.
"SOMETHING is over there in the
woods," said the small camper
in a squeaky voice.
The bears ducked down.
"Just an owl," said the big camper.
The small one shined the flashlight.
But he missed the cubs.
"Maybe raccoons?" said the middle one.
The small one said,
"I KNOW it was BEARS!"
"Oh yeah?" said the big one.
"Where are they?"
The campers went into their tent.

34

"Funny, I can't zip the flap,"
said the middle one. "It's stuck!
That means SOMETHING
could get in."
"Not to worry," said the big one.

36

At last the flashlights went out.

The moon crept slowly up the sky.

Bats swooped low.

The owl *who-who-whooed.*

The bears could hear little rumbles

like small growls coming

from the tent.

6.
MARSHMALLOWS!

"NOW!" said Sassy.

The cubs climbed on the picnic table.

Sassy tore open a box.

Lum pried the lid off the cooler.

"MARSHMALLOWS!" said Sassy.

The cubs put marshmallows on sticks
and stuck them in the coals.

They got black and gooey.

"Yum," said Lum.

"Double yum," said Sassy.

Sassy found a bottle of red goop.

Lum found a bottle of yellow goop.

Sassy squirted red on the table.

She squirted the cooler.

Lum squirted yellow on the bench.

He aimed at the boxes.

Sassy squirted Lum in the nose.

"YUCK!" he said.

Lum squirted Sassy's ear.

"DOUBLE YUCK!" she said.

The bears heard a loud GROWL.

"Yipes! It's Mother!" said Lum.

"We're gonna get it!"

The small camper heard it too.

"BEARS!" he shouted from his tent.

"Hear that growl? BEARS!"

He aimed his flashlight at the table.

"SOMETHING is on our picnic table.

AND THERE THEY ARE!" he cried.

Sassy and Lum jumped off the table.

They ran as fast as their
stubby legs could go.
The raccoon twins jumped
on the table.
They started licking the red
and yellow goop.
The middle camper cried,
"BEARS? BEARS IN CAMP?"
The small camper aimed his bright
light at the picnic table.
The raccoon twins hurried off.
They left red and yellow pawprints.
"THERE are your BEARS!"
said the big camper.
He came out of the tent.
"Two raccoons! And what a mess!"

Mother Bear was waiting in the bushes.

"What bad bears!" she growled.

"I told you—BEWARE of campers.

You never know WHAT they will do!"

The three bears hurried home.

Sassy and Lum were sent

straight to bed without any supper.

"Now no one believes him," said Sassy.

"And we got him in trouble too."

On Sunday, Mother Bear was busy.

Sassy and Lum hurried to the lake.

The three campers

were packing the car.

They tied the boat on the top.

Then they started to drive away.

The small camper was looking out
the back window.

"NOW!" said Sassy.

"YES!" said Lum.

The bear cubs came out of the bushes.

They waved their paws.

The small camper waved back.

Then he held a black box to his face.

A light flashed!

The bears blinked.

"CAMPERS!" said Sassy.

"You never know WHAT they will do,"
said Lum.

KAY WINTERS is the author of several books for children, including *Did You See What I Saw?: Poems About School; Wolf Watch;* and *The Teeny Tiny Ghost.* She lives with her husband in Quakertown, Pennsylvania.

BRIAN LIES has illustrated many children's books, including the Flatfoot Fox mystery series and *Hamlet and the Enormous Chinese Dragon Kite,* which he also wrote. He lives with his family in an old farmhouse in eastern Massachusetts.